2008

MAR - - 2013

cu Jan/10

	DATE DUE		

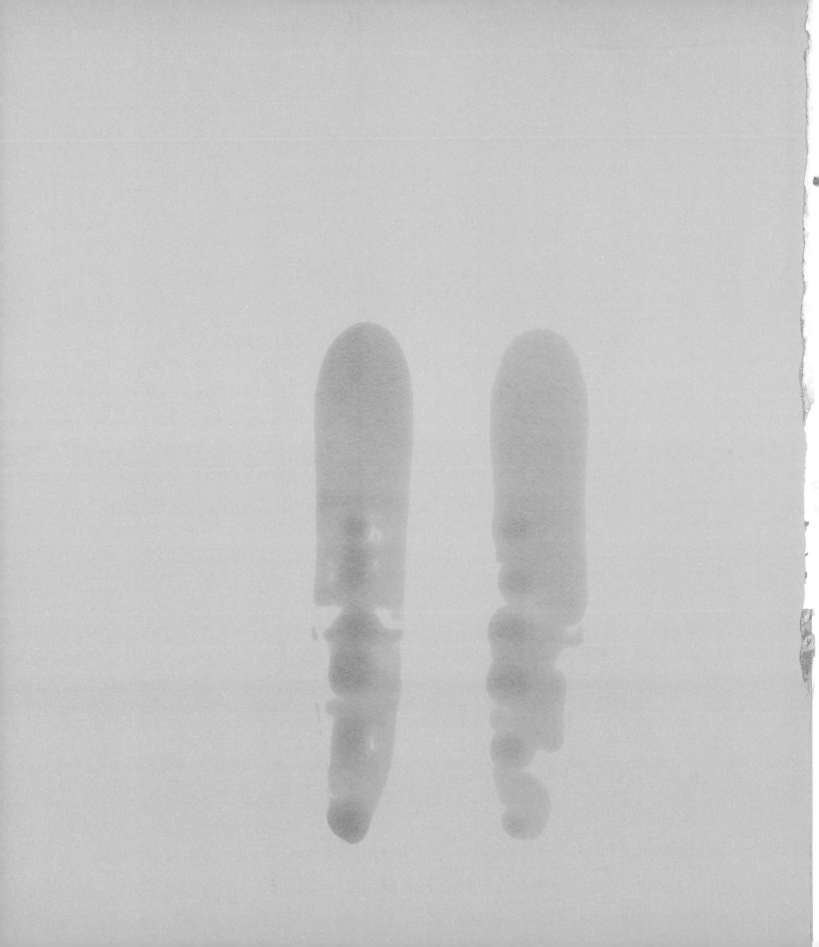

PUFFLING

WHAT IS A PUFFLING?

A puffling is a baby puffin. Although puffins and penguins look a lot alike, a puffin is not a penguin. Puffins live in the Northern Hemisphere and can fly, and penguins live in the Southern Hemisphere and cannot fly.

Puffins' bills are striped and colorful, so people have given them nicknames like Sea Parrot and Clown of the Sea. Puffins spend most of their lives in water, coming to land once a year to hatch a puffling, and they live in burrows they dig with their bills and feet. Parent puffins make puffling nests out of feathers and grass. The mother puffin lays one egg each year, and both parents help keep the egg warm and raise the chick. Puffins' favorite food is small fish, and parents feed their pufflings several times a day. The little pufflings grow to be about one foot tall, and weigh about a pound.

When puffins are ready to leave their nests, they go out to the ocean and stay there until they are two or three years old. Then, they return to the same area where they were hatched. Puffins live to be about twenty years old, and they keep the same partner their whole lives.

For Olivia, Jillian and Gwennie—M.W.
For Angus, Hugo and Freya—J.V.

A Feiwel and Friends Book
An Imprint of Macmillan

Library of Congress Cataloging-in-Publication Data

Wild, Margaret,
Puffling / Margaret Wild ; illustrated by Julie Vivas. — 1st ed.   p. cm.
Summary: As his affectionate parents nourish and protect him, a plucky young puffin impatiently waits—but not without some reservations—for the day when he is "strong enough and tall enough and brave enough" to leave his nest on the rocky cliff-face and waddle off to the sea.

ISBN: 978-0-312-56570-1
[1. Puffins—Fiction. 2. Growth—Fiction. 3. Parent and child—Fiction.]
I. Vivas, Julie, ill. II. Title.
PZ7.W64574Pu 2009   [E]—dc22   2008048137

Originally published in Australia by Omnibus Books, an imprint of Scholastic Australia Pty Ltd

Julie Vivas used pastel and watercolor pencil on textured paper for the illustrations for this book. Book design by Eija Murch-Lempinen.

Feiwel and Friends logo designed by Filomena Tuosto

First U.S. Edition: 2009

10 9 8 7 6 5 4 3 2 1

www.feiwelandfriends.com

PUFFLING

Margaret
WILD

Julie
VIVAS

Feiwel and Friends
New York

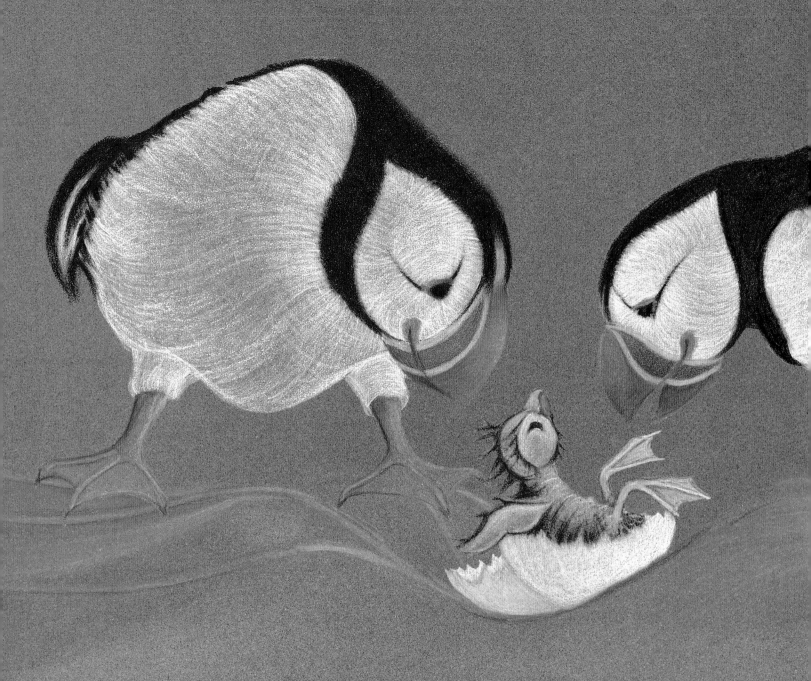

In summer, when the light is soft and
night never truly falls, the egg hatched.

"Hello, Puffling!" said the parents,
Big Stripy Beak and Long Black Feather.

Puffling was small and soft—and very hungry, so every day, Big Stripy Beak and Long Black Feather took turns to go fishing.

They said, "There are scary gulls out there, watching and waiting. Stay put in the burrow, Puffling, and we'll bring you back good things to eat."

So Puffling stayed put.

And every day, Big Stripy Beak or Long
Black Feather brought him back fish
and sand-eels.

One evening Puffling asked,
"Big Stripy Beak and Long Black
Feather, when will I leave
the burrow?"

"When you are strong enough
and tall enough and brave
enough, you'll leave
the burrow all by
yourself," said
Big Stripy Beak.
"You'll waddle off
into the dark as fast
as you can so the scary
gulls can't catch you."

"Then you'll jump off the cliff into the water and paddle away," said Long Black Feather.
"You'll find friends and you'll swim and sleep in the swell of the sea until it's time to come back home."

Puffling jumped up and down.

He couldn't wait!

The next morning Puffling asked,

"Am I strong enough yet?"

Long Black Feather watched him paddle his feet.

"Nearly," she said.

"Am I tall enough yet?" asked Puffling.

Big Stripy Beak measured his height.

"Not quite," he said.

"Am I brave enough yet?"
asked Puffling.

Big Stripy Beak and Long Black
Feather listened to his heart.

"Almost," they said.

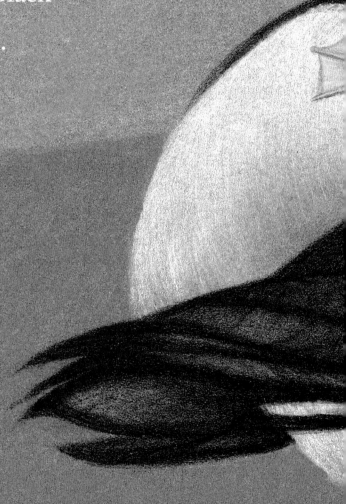

As the weeks went past,
Puffling grew bigger and bolder.

He popped his head out
of the burrow.

He stuck one leg out of
the burrow.

He waggled his bottom at the
scary gulls, watching and waiting.

But he remembered
never to go right out
of the burrow.

One evening Puffling said, "Big Stripy Beak and Long Black Feather, am I strong enough and tall enough and brave enough yet to leave the burrow?"

Long Black Feather watched him paddle his feet. "Perfect," she said.

Big Stripy Beak measured his height. "Just right," he said.

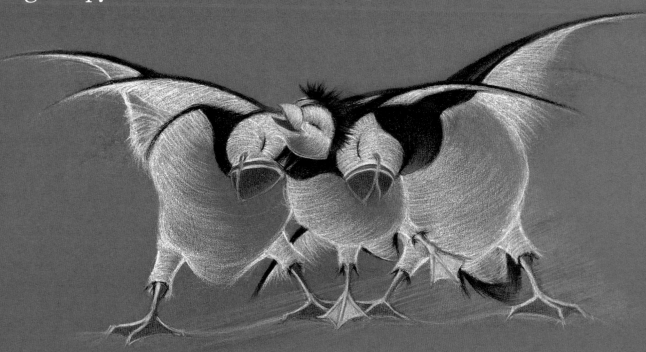

Then they held Puffling close, and listened to his heart.

It beat as loudly and powerfully as the ocean waves.

"Yes!" said Big Stripy Beak and Long Black Feather.
"You are strong enough and tall enough and brave
enough to leave the burrow."

Puffling felt happy, but a bit sad, too.
"Good-bye, Big Stripy Beak and Long Black Feather,"
he said, rubbing his beak against theirs.

"One more rub!" said Big Stripy Beak.

"Two more rubs!" said Long Black Feather.

As they flew away, they called, "You'll be our dear Puffling—
even when you're grown-up and have a chick of your own."

Puffling was alone now, but he stood straight
and tall. He looked out of the burrow into
the darkening night. Somewhere out there
were the scary gulls, watching and waiting.

He waddled. He waddled as fast as
he could, along the cliff path.
And just as the scary gulls swooped . . .

he plunged into the sea and paddled away

with his new friends.

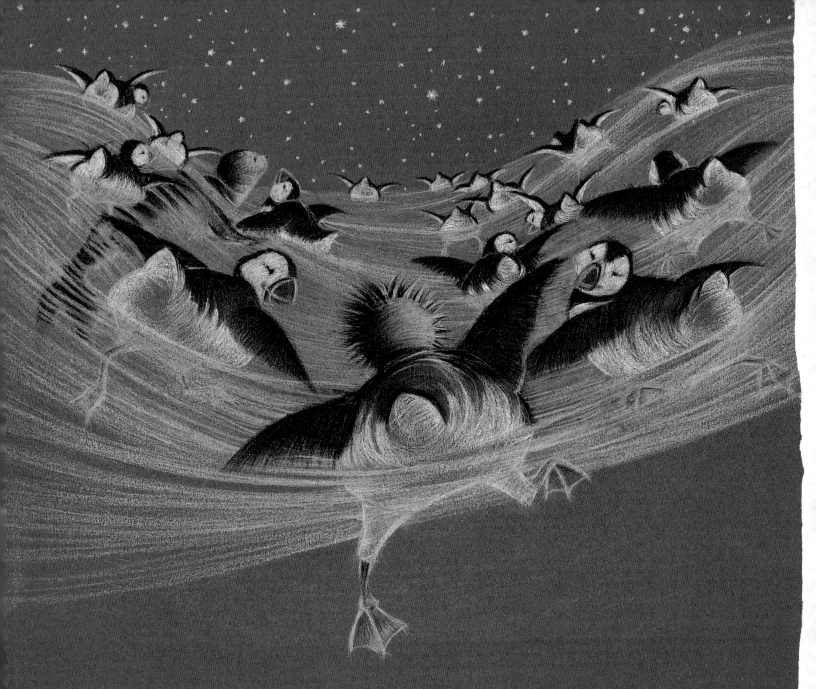

One day, he'd come back home and make his own
burrow. And when his own egg hatched, he'd think
of Big Stripy Beak and Long Black Feather and
say, "Hello, little Puffling!"